FAVOURITE Adventure STORIES

An illustrated treasury

LITTLE TIGER

LONDON

Contents

Princess Penelope And The Dragon

Written by Ellie Hattie

Illustrated by Tim Budgen

Princess Penelope And The Dragon

It was the summer holidays and Princess Penelope was bored.

"I'm bored, bored, bored," she huffed. "What can I do?"

"Have you swum in the moat?" suggested the Queen. Penelope nodded.

"Have you climbed to the top of the tallest turret?" asked the King. "Or played piggyback races with the knights?"

"I've done all those things," grumbled Penelope, "and I'm still bored."

"Why don't you try reading a book?" said the Queen.

"A book!" whooped Penelope. "Why didn't I think of that? What a BRILLIANT idea!" And she raced off to the library.

The shelves of the castle library were full to bursting with books on everything from archery and arithmetic to zombies and zoology. But on this particular morning Penelope decided to visit the maps section. She pulled out a book, opened the covers and – goodness me, what a surprise – there in front of her was a map of her very own kingdom!

"There are the Terribly Tall Mountains!" she cried excitedly. "And that's the Restless River that flows straight through the Ferocious Forest." Then something strange caught her eye. In the furthest, farthest corner of the map there was an 'X' and under it someone had scribbled in scritchy scratchy writing: HERE BE DRAGONS!

"I'd never be bored if I had a dragon for a friend," declared Penelope. "I must go and find one!" Penelope stuffed her backpack with:
• a torch
• some marshmallows
• a packet of biscuits
• her hairbrush and ribbons (which everyone knows are dragon-hunting essentials) and raced out of the castle door clutching the map.

"I'm off to find a dragon!" she called to the King and Queen.

"Righto," shouted the King over his newspaper. "Have fun!"

"Make sure you're home for tea!" called the Queen. The castle was a teeny tiny dot on the horizon when Penelope reached a rickety wooden bridge over the Restless River.

She was halfway across when, "Who's that tippy-tapping over MY bridge?" boomed a voice. Towering over Penelope stood a terrifying troll.

"This is my bridge and only I can use it!" he roared.

"Excuse me, Mr Troll," said Penelope in her sternest voice. "Don't you know it's terribly rude not to share?"

"What's sharing?" asked the troll, peering through the straggly hair that hung over his eyes.

"Sharing," said Penelope, pulling her hairbrush and ribbons out of her backpack, "is *me* letting *you* use *my* brush to comb *your* hair. And then giving you some of my ribbons to tie it out of the way."

When Penelope had finished the troll looked rather handsome.

"Oh, thank you," he beamed, admiring his reflection in the stream. "Would you like to use my bridge, now?"

"Yes, please, Mr Troll," said Penelope as she tippy-tapped over the bridge. "Now I can carry on looking for a dragon."

"Dragon? Here?" asked the troll in alarm. "You can't leave me on my own if there are dragons around!"

"Well you'd better come with me then," replied Penelope, and off she trotted with the troll following nervously after her.

By lunchtime they had reached the Ferocious Forest. It was dark beneath the trees and the rustling leaves sounded like whispering voices.

"I don't like the dark," trembled the troll (who was not nearly as terrifying as he looked).

Penelope didn't either, so she switched on her torch. The light shone into the wood and there, standing on the path in front of them, was a hairy scary wolf. He had sharp teeth, terrifying eyes and his tummy went *rumble grumble rumble*.

"I think he's hungry!" whispered the troll. "And I think he wants to eat us!"

"Fiddlesticks!" cried Penelope. "Why would he eat us when he could eat these!" And she pulled out her packet of biscuits.

When the wolf had gobbled up every last crumb he didn't look quite so ferocious. And when Penelope and the troll carried on walking, the wolf padded silently after them.

"I think he wants to find a dragon too!" smiled Penelope.

"Well, he won't have long to wait," wailed the troll, pointing to a large footprint and a charred tree. Just then a drop of water plopped onto his head. "I do believe it's started to rain. Perhaps we ought to go home," the troll added hopefully.

Penelope looked up at the sky. "Erm, that's not rain," she said. Standing over them was a huge red dragon crying enormous, salty tears.

"Dear me," said Penelope, patting the dragon's foot. "Whatever is the matter?"

"Nobody wants to be my friend," snuffled the dragon. "All I do is set fire to things and that's no good for anything."

"Stuff and nonsense!" said Penelope sternly.

16

"Firstly, I've been searching for a dragon especially to be my friend and secondly, if you would kindly breathe on these branches I'll show you the very best thing you can do with a fire."

Penelope pulled out four marshmallows from her bag and put them onto four twigs. They all held them over the bonfire's flames and, when they were soft and melty, she showed everyone how to gobble them up without dribbling any gooey marshmallow goodness.

"Can I have another one, please?" asked the dragon happily when he'd finished slurping his marshmallow.

"Absolutely not!" cried Penelope. "You'll spoil your appetite, and it's nearly tea time! Would you be kind enough to give us a lift home, please?"

"Of course!" cheered the dragon as the troll, the wolf and Princess Penelope clambered onto his back.

There was a slight commotion when they returned to the castle but pretty soon Princess Penelope had convinced the King and Queen to let her new friends stay. Everyone agreed that the troll made an excellent royal hairdresser, and although the King was irritable when the wolf ate his biscuits, and the Queen wasn't best pleased when the dragon singed her rosebushes, life was certainly interesting, and there was never a dull or boring day ever, ever again.

Finn's Igloo

Written by Emily Hibbs

Illustrated by Louise Wright

Finn's Igloo

Finn flipped the washing-up bowl upside down and turned the block of snow out. He lifted the newly-formed brick and slotted it in to the side of his igloo. Mum waved from the kitchen window and Finn grinned back. It was nearly finished!

Snow had fallen every day during the school holidays, and Finn had been hoping it would get deep enough to build an igloo. Then when he woke on Monday morning, it was up to the top of the cat flap! He'd been building the ice house for days – using instructions from a book Grandad had given him last Christmas.

Finn placed the last brick on top to finish the roof, and stood back to admire his work. The igloo was a bit wonky and quite small – but he was proud of it anyway. The kitchen window opened and Mum leaned out.

"It looks great!" she called. Finn could hear the phone ringing inside. "I'll come and visit in a minute."

Finn sighed. Mum was brilliant but she was busy working and she didn't have much time for snowball fights. The snow would have been much more fun if Finn's friends had been around to play with, but all the roads werc blocked.

Getting down on his hands and knees, Finn crawled inside his igloo. It was surprisingly warm! "I wish my friends were here to see," Finn thought to himself.

Then he heard someone stomping through the snow – Mum must have come to see the igloo! Finn crawled outside, then stopped and gasped. Where was his garden? What was going on?

The wooden fence and familiar street were gone. His igloo was perched on the side of a snowy mountain! Further down the slope, Finn could see a forest, and beyond, the ocean. The bright blue water seemed to go on forever. Finn blinked. Was he dreaming?

"Hello?" a voice said, sounding as shocked as Finn felt. Finn stood up. A boy around his own age was facing him. He was wearing a thick coat and huge leathery boots. He looked odd, but very warm!

"Hello," Finn said nervously. The boy looked Finn up and down. Finn had a funny feeling that the boy found his clothes strange, too.

"Do you live here? On the mountain?" asked the boy. "I'm Ila – I live down in the valley."

"I'm Finn," he replied, then shook his head. "No, I live —" A huge bird shrieked above them. Finn watched in amazement as it swooped toward the forest. "Wow!" he gasped.

"Quick!" cried Ila, running over to the toboggan he had left nearby. "It's a bald eagle – let's follow it! Jump on!"

Finn swung his legs over and grasped his new
friend round the waist. Before he knew it
they were off, racing down the mountain.
The snow whipped up around them
and Finn laughed in delight.
This was brilliant!

In front of them, he could see a cluster of igloos, much bigger than his
own. Some of them were even connected by tunnels!

"Is that where you live?" Finn called.

"Yep," Ila shouted back. "My igloo is the one with the canoe outside!"
But he was steering the toboggan away from the village, toward the ocean.
The boys jumped over ditches and veered around tree stumps.

Soon, they were out on smoother ice near the edge of the ocean. The water reflected the bright blue sky and was dotted with hundreds of little ice islands. Ila tugged on the rope and their toboggan came to a halt. Finn stepped off and immediately slipped over.

"Careful!" said Ila, helping him up. "You have to glide over the ice. Like this!"

Ila slid one foot across the slippery surface, then the other, finishing with a neat spin. Finn got to his feet, his legs wobbly. Taking cautious steps, he soon found his balance and skated over the ice. Finn and Ila looped around each other, laughing.

They pulled the toboggan back towards the forest where the snow was powdery - perfect for snowball fights! Finn and Ila raced between the trees, dodging each other's snowballs.

"Can I try on your coat?" Finn asked, as they stopped to rest.

Ila tugged off his enormous coat and Finn put it on, pulling the hood up over his head. It was very cosy and smelled of earth.

Ila tried on Finn's coat, too, peering curiously at the zip as Finn did it up.

"I should go home," Finn said at last. "It's getting dark and Mum will be worried about where I've got to."

"To your igloo?" asked Ila. Finn nodded.

"Come on," Ila called, leading them to where a reindeer stood beside a tree. Finn was so excited - a real reindeer! Ila tied the toboggan to its harness and they clambered on, heading back up the mountain.

By the time they
reached Finn's igloo, stars dotted
the sky and a ribbon of purple and green light danced
above them. "Wow!" Finn cried, gazing upwards.

"I've had so much fun today," Ila said, smiling.

"Me, too," said Finn. He hugged Ila tightly. "Goodbye!"

"Will you come and play with me again?"

"Well, I've got to go to school on Monday," said Finn, getting down on his hands and knees and crawling into the tunnel. "But that means I still have three days to come and play, if the snow lasts." His voice echoed inside the igloo. "Maybe we can build a snowman! See you tomorrow . . ."

"Finn!" Finn whirled round to see his mum peering into the igloo, smiling. Finn could see his front garden behind her. He was home!

Mum squeezed in through the tunnel. "I'm so impressed! It's magical in here!"

Finn hugged his mum tight and laughed – she had no idea just how magical it was!

Silver's Secret

Written by Gwen Bishop

Illustrated by Richard Watson

Silver's Secret

Ada's dog, Silver, had a patch over one eye and hot stinky breath. If you buried your nose deep into his fur, you could smell the sea - which was pretty much the only interesting thing about him. Ada wanted a dog like Pierrot, her friend Coco's dog. Pierrot was small and cute, and could beg for biscuits and jump through hula hoops.

"We need a new dog," announced Ada at breakfast. "Silver is too old and boring to play with me."

"I'm even older than Silver and I can still play," laughed Dad, chasing her around the kitchen. "Anyway, Silver is a very special dog, even if he sometimes seems a bit boring. Just you wait and see."

So Ada sat and watched Silver all day. She stared at him while he snoozed on the warm patch on the kitchen floor, while he snored in the living room and when he dozed on the flowerbeds in the garden.

By the end of the day, Silver had eaten one can of dog food, barked twice at the neighbour's cat and slept a LOT. He hadn't done anything even remotely exciting.

Watching Silver all day had made Ada very tired. And very bored. "Told you so," she yawned at bedtime when Dad came to tuck her in. "Silver is no fun at all."

"We'll see," smiled Dad. He kissed Ada on the forehead and she snuggled down in bed and fell fast asleep.

A little past midnight, Ada was woken up by the *click click* of claws on the kitchen floor. The back door gave a soft bump as something slipped outside. "Is someone there?" whispered Ada.

Silver's dog basket was empty. How strange! "Silver?" said Ada, quickly stuffing her feet into her wellies and creeping downstairs and out into the dark garden. Only it didn't look like her garden at all! The lawn was now a big, dark sea and waves lapped at the flowerbeds. Ada's mouth fell open. There in front of her, was a HUGE pirate ship!

It had black sails that billowed in the breeze and shadowy figures stood on the deck. They were very short, and very hairy. And one most definitely had a patch over his eye.

"Silver!" Ada cried. "What are you doing?"

"Woof!" barked Silver, wagging his tail. Standing next to him was a sausage dog with a peg leg, an enormous mongrel and a very fierce looking pug. They were all wearing pirate hats!

"Are you a . . . a . . . pirate?" stuttered Ada.

"Arr-ruff!" barked Captain Silver grandly, puffing out his chest. Ada suddenly felt very shy. She had never met a pirate dog before. But Silver gave her a smelly lick to reassure her and nosed Ada on to the ship.

"Right," giggled Ada when she had said hello to all of the pirate dogs. "Where are we going?"

Silver gave a few short barks and the doggy crew leapt into action. They lifted the anchor and sailed out on to the dark, black sea. As the ship raced over the waves, Silver let Ada climb up high onto the crow's nest. Then Ada helped Frank the sausage dog scrub the deck. The dogs weren't much like proper pirates – they chased seagulls, howled at the moon, "Arrrr-oooo-OOOOO!" and kept asking Ada to scratch their bellies.

When they reached a desert island, Ada and the pirate dogs jumped into the sea and doggy-paddled to the shore. Yipping and yapping, the dogs ran along the beach and Ada threw coconuts for Silver to fetch.

"Come on!" cried Ada. "Let's dig for treasure!"

Silver found a bone, Pickle the fierce pug dug up a boot and Ada found the best thing of all . . . a huge treasure chest! Inside the chest were golden, glowing . . ."Doggy biscuits!" giggled Ada.

Just then, there was a low and fearsome "Meeeeooowww!" Standing in front of them was a very mean-looking bunch of pirate cats! The dogs whimpered as one particularly fierce cat stalked forward. He had thick, snowy white fur, a squashed nose and a very scary scowl.

"Tiddles!" gasped Ada. It was the neighbour's cat, and Fluffy Tiddles and his crew were up to no good!

The cats darted forward and snatched the treasure. Frank the sausage dog tried to stop them, but he was too slow and small. Then Zack the mongrel and Pickle the pug gave chase but the cats turned and biffed them on their noses!

"Arr-Ooow!" they yelped. The mean moggies were getting away!

"Stop them, Silver!" cried Ada.

Silver jumped forward and gave his loudest and best pirate dog "GRRRRRRRRRR!" It scared the cats so much that they dropped the treasure at once and ran away!

"You did it!" cheered Ada, giving Silver a big hug. Pickle, Frank and Zack wagged their tails and licked Ada's face. Then they all helped carry the treasure and put it safely on the ship.

"That was the best adventure ever," Ada sighed, as they sailed home. "Can we go on another one soon?"

"Woof," agreed Silver, nuzzling her hand.

Ada woke up very early the next morning, fizzing with excitement. She raced downstairs. Silver was fast asleep in his doggy bed, but the silly dog had forgotten to take his pirate hat off! Ada gently lifted it off his head and kissed him.

"I'm sorry I doubted you Silver. You're the best, most exciting dog in the world," she whispered to Silver as he let out a loud doggy snore.

Marvin The Miniature Astronaut

Written by Georgiana Deutsch

Illustrated by Erica Salcedo

Marvin The Miniature Astronaut

"Shooting stars!" yelped Marvin the mouse, almost knocking over his miniature telescope as he rushed to his bedroom window. "That's GINORMOUS! Mum! Dad!" he called, leaping down the stairs. "There's a new rocket in the Space Centre! Maybe they're looking for astronauts to fly it!"

"I think you'd make a brilliant astronaut, Marvin," smiled his mum. "But try not to get your hopes up. Mice are just too small to go into space!"

"Don't be long!" called Marvin's dad, as Marvin raced out of the door. "We're having cheese for dinner!"

As Marvin scampered across the road to see the gleaming silver rocket, he noticed a brightly coloured flyer fluttering on the ground.

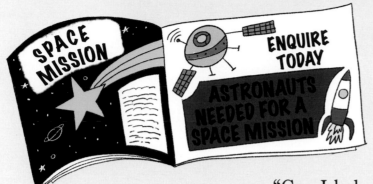

"Jumping Jupiter!" Marvin gasped. "I was right!" And he rushed into the Space Centre at once.

"Can I help you?" barked a loud voice.

Marvin looked up to see a large and rather grumpy-looking dog in a spacesuit frowning down at him.

"Yes!" squeaked Marvin. "I'd like to join your space mission!"

The dog's eyebrows shot up in surprise. "But you're a mouse!" he laughed. "You're far too small to be an astronaut!" And with that, he promptly turned back to his snack.

"I may be a mouse," Marvin replied, "but I know lots about space. And I'd bring heaps of cheese!"

"Cheese?" replied the dog, holding out his paw. "Why didn't you say so? I'm Space Commander Spike. Be here at sunrise tomorrow. And don't forget the cheese!"

Marvin dashed home, feeling as though he might burst with happiness.

"Well done, lad!" called Marvin's dad, as Marvin raced to pack a bag of essential space supplies:

• Cheese

• Cheese

• More cheese (just in case)

The next morning, Marvin's whiskers were quivering with excitement as he reported to Space Commander Spike.

"Ah, Marvin!" barked Spike. "Follow me. We've had a special spacesuit made for you – extra small!"

As Marvin followed Spike into the rocket, he blinked in amazement. It was incredible!

"Marvin, I'd like to introduce you to our team of astronauts. Meet Bizz and Buzz," said Spike. Two identical black cats looked up from their space map and purred. "This is Professor Moon." Spike gestured towards a bespectacled owl. "Professor Moon is our computer whizz! And most important of all, this is our computer." Space Commander Spike pointed at a huge machine that whirred and clicked in the centre of the room.

Marvin could hardly contain his excitement as he pulled on his spacesuit.

"Right, everyone!" called Spike, closing the spaceship door. "We're ready to launch! Now, Marvin, you just stay out of the way and keep the cheese . . . I mean, yourself, safe. 5 . . . 4 . . . 3 . . . 2 . . . 1 . . . BLAST OFF!"

Marvin felt a whoosh of delight as the rocket shot up into space. Soon he could see stars and planets out of the window. At last he was a real astronaut!

Then suddenly there was a loud BANG! The lights in the spaceship flickered and a warning alarm sounded.

"Oh NO!" Spike exclaimed. "It's a problem with the computer! If we don't fix it, we'll never get home again!"

"Impossible!" hooted Professor Moon, indignantly. "I built that computer – it can't be broken!"

"Perhaps this might help to restart it?" suggested Bizz, pressing a large blue button.

"That's not the restart button!" squawked Professor Moon, as jelly beans flew into the air. "That's the emergency sweets dispenser!"

"THIS should fix it," said Buzz, confidently putting her paws on a yellow button. SQUELCH! An enormous squirt of green goo shot out of the computer and straight into Professor Moon's face. Marvin tried very hard not to giggle.

"Keep calm!" shouted Spike. "I can get us out of this pickle." But as Spike raced over to Professor Moon, he slipped in the green slime and crashed into a bright red button. WHOOSH!

Marvin felt his tummy swoop as he floated up out of his seat. He looked around in alarm to see all the astronauts drifting around the spaceship.

"Oh no!" called Spike, trying to catch the floating jelly beans as Bizz turned somersaults in the air. "That was the gravity button!"

"Galloping galaxies!" thought Marvin, quickly grabbing on to the computer to stop himself floating away. "There must be a way of fixing this!" And just then, Marvin saw it – there was a hole in the corner of the computer – and inside was something VERY strange!

"Surely not!" whispered Marvin, twitching his nose as a familiar scent wafted towards him. "It's coming from inside the computer!"

Marvin squeezed himself through the hole, following the distinctive smell. And there, wedged amongst all the wires, was a piece of CHEESE!

Marvin couldn't believe his eyes! Whiskers trembling, he took a huge breath and grabbed the cheese. He pulled with all his might until . . . POP! Marvin and the cheese flew back out of the computer. The alarm had stopped sounding, the lights were back on and the astronauts were lying in a heap on the floor, looking at Marvin in amazement.

"This cheese was blocking the computer!" squeaked Marvin excitedly.

"But what on earth was it doing there?" frowned Professor Moon, ruffling his feathers.

"Oh THAT'S where my emergency piece of cheese went!" cried Spike, looking at it greedily. "I've been looking for that everywhere . . ."

"Well!" smiled Bizz and Buzz. "Thank goodness Marvin was here to save the day!"

"Hurrah for Marvin the miniature astronaut!" they all cheered as Marvin beamed with pride.

"Yes!" roared Space Commander Spike, his mouth full of cheese. "Let's all have extra helpings of cheese to celebrate!"

Benji And The Aliens

Written by Ellie Hattie

Illustrated by Becky Down

Benji And The Aliens

It was a perfectly ordinary Saturday morning. Granny was busy baking in the kitchen and the sweet smell of fresh bread and was wafting up the stairs. Benji hopped out of bed; there was nothing nicer than Granny's bread and homemade jam for breakfast. He was pulling on his socks when CRASH beep WALLOP BANG fizzle wizzle POP! there was a commotion in the back garden!

Benji raced to the window. Sitting in the middle of Granny's vegetable patch was a spaceship. "WOWSERS TROUSERS!" cried Benji.

"Woof, woof, woof!" yapped Spot the dog, who had come to see what the fuss was about.

Benji and Spot watched in shock as three small aliens waddled down the gang plank. The aliens were bright green. They each had three stumpy legs, six googly eyes and two long tickle arms which they were using to pick and eat Granny's prize-winning tomatoes!

"STOP!" cried Benji through the window. "Granny! There are aliens in the garden, and they're eating your tomatoes!"

"Really?" Granny called up the stairs. "Well, can you ask them to leave some for afternoon tea? I'm just popping out to borrow some flour from Mrs Prendergast. Back soon!" The front door closed with a click.

"C'mon, Spot," said Benji, running down the stairs and yanking on his wellie boots. "We'd better go and stop these aliens!"

By the time they made it outside the aliens had moved on to Granny's lettuces. "Hey!" said Benji.

"Hey! Hey! Hey!" replied the aliens through a mouthful of leaves.

"Look, you can't just land in someone's garden and help yourself to their salad!" said Benji. Spot wagged his tail in agreement.

The aliens looked confused. They offered a large leaf to Benji. "Nom, nom, nom?" they asked.

"No, no, no!" replied Benji. "Who's in charge here? Can you take me to your leader?" The aliens looked at each other. Then they looked at Benji. Before you could say 'Not on your nellie' the aliens had whisked Benji and Spot into the spaceship! The doors closed. The engines started. And the ship shot upwards, out of the garden and into outer space.

"Cool!" cried Benji as he watched the earth disappear behind them. Then he turned to inspect the ship. It was full of beeping buzzers, flashing lights and screens showing pictures of incredible foods! "Is your leader here?" Benji asked the biggest of the small aliens who, according to the name on his badge, was called Timmy.

"No, no, no!" giggled Timmy, thrusting a piece of paper into Benji's hand. Benji looked at the flyer. It said:

Welcome, traveller, to the Interstellar Culinary Cruise!
Tantalise your tastebuds with food
from around the universe!

"Good job we didn't eat breakfast, Spot!" smiled Benji as the ship sped towards its first stop.

Timmy and the two other aliens (who were called Tina and Tony) landed the ship on a big yellow planet. They pulled flippers onto their feet and flapped down the gang plank, with Benji and Spot waddling behind. The whole planet was a swirling pool of yellow gloop!

"Splish, splash, splosh!" cried the aliens as they dived straight in and started slurping. Spot wagged his tail and raced after them.

"Wait for me!" called Benji as he jumped in too. To his surprise, the gloop tasted scrumptiously familiar. "CUSTARD!" he cried. And it wasn't just any custard. It was the most deliciously creamy, milky, wondrous custard he'd ever had. "Amazing!" Benji beamed.

The five friends drank as much custardy gloop as their tummies could take and then they rolled themselves back onto the ship. "Up, up, up!" laughed Tina as she sailed the ship on to the next stop on the tour.

In the Banana Nebula they feasted on long, thin, stripy fruits. Each stripe was a different flavour. "It's like a whole meal in one mouthful!" giggled Benji.

They stopped off at an asteroid belt where they nibbled on rocky outcrops that fizzed and popped like sweet fireworks in Benji's mouth. "Ooh! That tickles!" Benji snorted, as Spot sneezed a sticky puppy sneeze.

The friends rocketed from planet to planet. They slurped soup from a comet's tail, drank lemonade from gushing waterfalls and munched on frozen yoghurt icecaps.

"Oooof, no more food thanks, I'm going to pop!" sighed Benji as he flumped on the floor of the spaceship. "I think you might have to take me home now, Granny will be wondering where I am!"

"Burp, burp, burp," agreed Timmy, Tina and Tony, rubbing their bulging bellies. CRASH beep WALLOP BANG fizzle wizzle POP went the spaceship as it landed back in Granny's garden.

"Benji, dear," cried Granny from the kitchen window, "you're just in time for afternoon tea! Can you bring in the rest of those tomatoes, please? Oh, and ask your friends to stay if you like – there's plenty to go round."

Granny had put on quite a spread. There were cupcakes and trifle. Prize-winning-tomato and cheese sandwiches. Buns with jam and fruit salad with cream.

"Yum, yum, yum, tum, tum, tum!" sang Timmy, Tina and Tony as they wolfed everything down hungrily – including some of Spot's dog biscuits.

When tea was finished and the plates were washed Benji, Spot and Granny waved goodbye to the aliens.

"Weren't they lovely?" smiled Granny. "I do hope they come again soon." Benji and Spot hoped they would too.

Which was lucky because the very next Saturday morning not one but three spaceships, and two flying saucers, landed with a whoosh WALLOP wizzle BANG crash bash POP in the garden.

"Wowsers!" said Benji as a horde of aliens in various shapes and sizes waddled and wobbled up the garden path. "I think we're going to need more cups."

"It appears my afternoon tea has become an intergalactic success!" chuckled Granny. And she was absolutely right!

Cowboy Mike
Starts School

Written by Georgiana Deutsch

Illustrated by Chris Jevons

Cowboy Mike Starts School

"Yee-ha!" cried Mike's mum as she lassoed his bag from the hallway. "Time for your first day at cowboy school!"

"Mum?" asked Mike, as he slipped his feet into his new, too-big cowboy boots. "What if I'm not very good at being a cowboy?"

"You'll be mighty fine," laughed Mum. "Just think of all that time you've spent practising! Don't forget, I'll be proud of you no matter what. Why don't you take Buckaroo with you to help you feel brave – that lazy hound could do with some exercise!"

Mike tried to smile as Buckaroo gave a sleepy snore but he couldn't help worrying. His mum and dad were the best cowboys in the West. What if he was no good? What if he let his whole family down?

As Buckaroo and Mike walked down the track to school, Mike waved to Chuck the train driver at the level crossing.

"Good luck, Mike!" called Chuck, as the train chuffed slowly past. "You'll do your parents proud!" Mike nodded nervously and tried to stop his knees from knocking together.

"Howdy, partners!" yelled the teacher, Big Jim, as Mike arrived at school. "I hope y'all are excited for your first day at cowboy school! Now, grab those lassos and let's see what you're made of!"

Mike joined the line, his hands shaking. He could hit the post every time at home, but when his turn came, Mike could feel the whole class watching him. What if he messed up in front of everyone? Mike gulped and glanced at Big Jim as he threw his lasso towards the post.

"Whoa!" cried Big Jim, as the lasso landed neatly around his waist. "Easy, Mike! You were supposed to be aiming for the post, not me!" Mike turned bright red. "Sorry, Big Jim," he mumbled, as he tried to ignore the giggles from his classmates. Mike looked around for reassurance from Buckaroo, but he was fast asleep under a tree. "Typical!" sighed Mike.

Next, it was the class's first horse riding lesson. Mike had been practising riding on a fence at home, so surely this wouldn't be too different. But as Mike sat in the saddle of a fat pony called Star, he realised just how high above the ground he was . . .

"Alrighty!" yelled Big Jim, at the top of his voice. "It's time to learn how to ride!"

Mike jumped in surprise and accidentally pulled on the reins. With a startled whinny, Star leaped into the air.

"Aaaaagh!" shouted Mike as he slid off the pony, right into the middle of a very juicy pile of horse dung. SQUELCH! Mike closed his eyes and sighed. He wished he was back at home playing horses with Buckaroo.

73

After lunch, it was time for a line dancing lesson. This was what Mike had been dreading all day. Everything he'd practised had gone wrong, and he'd never even tried dancing.

"Run up to the line, everyone!" called Big Jim. "Five, six, seven, eight!" Mike leapt forwards and started to dance. As he tapped his heels and twirled on the spot, Mike broke into a huge grin. He couldn't believe it . . . he was actually quite good! Mike skipped backwards happily and linked arms with his classmates. But as they danced in a long line, Mike suddenly stumbled. He tripped over his too-big boots, and felt his legs disappear from underneath him as he lost his balance. As he flew through the air, he realised the whole line was falling with him . . .

With a huge crash, Mike and his classmates landed in a tangled heap on the floor.

"This has been the worst first day of cowboy school ever!" thought Mike, as everyone dusted themselves off. "Even Buckaroo must be ashamed of me!" he muttered, realising that his dog was nowhere to be seen.

At last, it was home time, but there was still no sign of Buckaroo. As Mike trudged along the railway track, he suddenly heard cries of panic. He looked up and gasped – Chuck's train was racing at breakneck speed towards the level crossing!

"It's a runaway train!" Big Jim shouted, waving his hat in the air.

"Look at that poor creature!" cried Miss Cranky, pointing at something on the tracks.

Mike peered in the direction she was pointing and, suddenly, he saw it . . . There, asleep on the tracks was Buckaroo! And the runaway train was

getting closer and closer! Mike grabbed his lasso, his heart pounding in his chest. He had to save Buckaroo! But could he do it, with all these people watching him? As he looked over at his faithful hound, Mike was filled with courage. He took aim and threw his lasso as far as he could. BINGO! The lasso landed neatly around Buckaroo. Mike heaved on the rope, but he wasn't strong enough to move the sleeping Buckaroo! Big Jim and old Mrs Cranky grabbed the rope, and the three of them pulled with all their might.

Suddenly, Mike felt Buckaroo starting to move. He looked over his shoulder to see the whole crowd pulling on the rope behind him! WHOOSH! The runaway train whizzed past, just as Buckaroo was pulled to safety.

Mike turned to his friends with a huge grin on his face. He'd saved Buckaroo's life! He threw his arms around him and couldn't help laughing – Buckaroo was still fast asleep!

"That dog could sleep through anything!" declared Big Jim, looking at Mike in amazement. "That was a cracking shot, Mike! You're going to be a fine cowboy!"

Just then, Chuck came running up. "Those pesky bandits stole my train!" he panted. "I've told the sheriff – he'll pick 'em up when they run out of fuel! Mike, you saved the day!"

"Mike's a hero!" shouted the crowd. Mike beamed with happiness. This had been the best first day at cowboy school ever!

"I think it's time for a celebration!" cheered Big Jim. "Everyone, follow me for a tip-top line dancing hoedown!"

80

My Best Friend Is A Superhero

Written by Becky Davies

Illustrated by Sharon Harmer

My Best Friend Is A Superhero

Alice was playing by herself in the park when she noticed a removal van outside number 27. She crossed the street at once and peered curiously through the window. There were boxes everywhere, and in one of them Alice could see a baseball cap and a stack of comic books. Written across the box in large letters was the name GEORGE.

Brilliant, she thought, *someone to play with!* Alice hoped this George would want to be her friend. Maybe even her BEST friend. She knocked on the door eagerly.

But when George's mum answered the door, she told Alice that George was out. Disappointed, Alice trudged back to the park alone.

She had been playing on the swings for half an hour when all of a sudden the hairs on the back of her neck stood up. She whirled around to see a small boy with sandy hair and glasses facing her. Where had he come from?

"Hello, I'm George," he said, looking at her timidly.

There was something unusual about him, but Alice couldn't put her finger on it. "Hello George, I'm Alice. Would you like to play?"

George was very nice once he had recovered from his shyness, and liked comic books almost as much as Alice did! He had the coolest ideas for games, and the two played together until the sun set. It wasn't until she was eating her supper that Alice realised what was strange about him – he had been wearing odd shoes!

Over the next few weeks Alice and George became firm friends. Alice liked George very much, though she noticed a few more things about him that were unusual. His clothes were *often* on back to front or inside out, as if he had got dressed in a hurry. Then there was the way he seemed to arrive from nowhere – Alice never heard or saw him approach, he just *appeared*. And not to mention the large rucksack that George always carried with him which he wouldn't EVER take off, not even when they were crossing the monkey bars to escape radioactive crocodiles! Alice liked that George was different, but other children had started to notice.

One day Alice was in the park when she heard the others talking about George. She shuffled closer to listen.

"Maybe he's a ninja," said Simon. "That would explain how he moves so quietly!"

"Or perhaps he's a werewolf!" Hannah suggested. "And he's up all night howling at the moon! Then he's so tired that he can't get dressed properly." They all giggled explosively.

"I've got it!" Simon cried. "He's a mad scientist! His bag is full of secret ingredients he doesn't want to leave at home!"

"But George isn't mad," Alice protested quietly.

They looked around, surprised.

"And I asked him to help me with my Science homework last week. He wasn't very good."

That could all be part of the disguise!" said Simon enthusiastically.

"Definitely not," said Alice firmly.

"Well, what then?" Simon demanded. "I bet you think he's some kind of superhero, like from your lame comics!" The group giggled again, and wandered off.

Alice stood very still, her brain working furiously. A superhero . . . of course!

George did often appear out of nowhere, and disappear just as quickly, like he had some kind of super-human ability. And maybe his clothes were dishevelled because he put them on in a hurry after changing out of his superhero outfit . . . Alice's mouth fell open. "I bet that's what's in the bag!"

Suddenly it all made sense. For days Alice could think of nothing else. She watched George closely – or as closely as you can watch someone who keeps disappearing – and after a week she was convinced. All she needed now was proof! But how would she get it?

When George arrived at the park that Saturday Alice was ready for him, waiting on top of the monkey bars. "Hi!" he called. "What are you doing up there?"

"I'm stuck!" Alice wailed, wobbling dramatically. "Help me, George!"

"Just climb down the same way you got up," said George, frowning.

"I need rescuing, George. I'm in danger!"

"Erm . . . " said George, scratching his head. "I'll go get your dad?"

Alice sighed. Of course it wouldn't be that easy. "Never mind. I think I can get down after all."

"I've got a great idea for a new game," said George, when Alice was back on the ground. "Want to hear it?"

"Maybe later," Alice replied impatiently. "How about I push you on the swings first?"

"OK," said George, shrugging.

Alice grinned. *All I have to do is push him high enough* she thought, *and he'll have no choice but to fly.* She began to push George, gently at first but then higher and higher.

"Woohoo!" he laughed. "Higher, Alice!"

"I can't push any harder," Alice grunted, sweat beading on her forehead.

With his backpack on George was *heavy*. "I give up!" she said. "What do you keep in this thing anyway, George?"

"My bag?" he chuckled, dragging his feet on the floor to stop the swing. "It's no big secret, it's just my swimming kit." He opened the bag, and showed Alice a pair of goggles, swimming trunks and a big blue towel.

"So you're not . . . a superhero?" asked Alice in a quiet voice.

George laughed. "Of course not! Why on earth did you think I was?"

Alice explained, and George fell about laughing. He only stopped giggling when he caught sight of Alice's face, which had gone bright red.

"Oh I'm sorry Alice. I suppose some of the things I do are a bit strange," he admitted. "I don't know why, but I can't help it. I hope you don't mind that I'm not a superhero."

Alice shook her head. "I don't mind one bit," she said.

"Even though I'm not cool?"

"I think that you are the coolest, best friend there is. Superhero or not," she said firmly.

Then one day, a few weeks later, Alice was racing back from her dance lesson when all of a sudden she tripped. She fell forwards sharply - straight into the busy road! Suddenly, she felt herself being lifted up into the air - she was flying in somebody's arms!

Before she knew it she was placed gently back on the ground. Alice turned around shakily to thank her rescuer. She couldn't see his eyes past the goggles he was wearing, and only caught a glimpse of sandy coloured hair before, with a swish of a bright blue cape, he was gone. But Alice knew for sure.

"I was right!" she said. "My best friend really is a superhero!" Alice smiled to herself as she walked slowly home, pausing in front of George's house where she could see a light in his bedroom window. "Thank you George!" she whispered. "Your secret's safe with me."

A Prehistoric Pet

Written by Georgiana Deutsch

Illustrated by Kim Barnes

A Prehistoric Pet

Tom grinned as he raced into the rescue centre. His parents had finally agreed that he could get a dog – as long as it helped to keep Tom's dad's prize-winning broccoli safe! With the village vegetable competition only a month away, and a gang of vegetable thieves on the loose, they couldn't take any chances.

"What about this clever chap?" asked Tom's mum, clapping her hands in delight at a spotty dog who was balancing a ball on the tip of its nose. "He'd be able to outwit any vegetable thieves."

"This one would make a brilliant guard dog!" shouted Tom's dad, as he patted a barking dog with very big teeth.

Tom wrinkled his nose uncertainly. None of these dogs was quite right.

Suddenly, a flash of colour caught Tom's eye. There, sitting quietly in the corner of the room, was the coolest dog Tom had ever seen! She was green and scaly and absolutely ginormous.

"That's the one!" cried Tom excitedly.

"An excellent choice!" said the owner of the rescue centre, hurrying over. "This is Mabel."

"Are you sure she's a dog?" asked Tom's mum, peering at the animal curiously. "She's a funny colour!"

"Oh yes," replied the rescue centre owner. "Someone found Mabel roaming around the woods, and we think she's a very rare breed! We've tried to find her a new home, but no one seems to want her."

"Well she certainly looks fierce," nodded Tom's dad, peering at the spikes on her tail. "And she's so big that her bark must be ferocious!"

That settled it, and Tom and Mabel climbed into the back of the car together. Mabel was so big that her spiky tail dangled out of the car window, but Tom beamed all the way home. He adored her already and couldn't wait to show her off.

The next morning, Tom raced straight into the garden to start teaching Mabel some tricks. As Mabel squeezed through the door, Tom couldn't help noticing that she looked even bigger than the day before.

"I thought your dad wanted a guard dog to scare off those vegetable thieves!" chuckled Mrs Peartree, the neighbour, as she peered nosily over the fence. "She doesn't look much like a dog to me! Can she at least do some good tricks?"

"Of course! Watch this!" Tom turned back to Mabel. "Sit, Mabel! Sit!" Tom stood on his tiptoes and held a treat above Mabel's nose. "Come on, girl," he whispered. "SIT!" But Mabel just blinked at Tom and waved her spiky tail.

Suddenly, Mrs Peartree's cat leaped onto the fence and hissed loudly at Mabel. Mabel looked very carefully at the cat, before lumbering towards Tom's dad's vegetable patch and starting to nibble on the runner beans.

"No, Mabel!" shouted Tom, sprinting after her. "Bad dog!"

"Tom! Come inside!" called his mum. "We've got something special for Mabel!"

"Steak!" Tom exclaimed, as he ran into the kitchen with Mabel barging clumsily after him. "Mabel will love that! Thanks, Mum!" But Mabel backed away from the steak, crashing noisily into the kitchen table.

"Careful, Mabel!" cried Tom's mum, as a pile of plates smashed onto the floor. "You're just too big for this kitchen!"

"Oh no!" frowned Tom's dad, looking up from his newspaper. "There's been ANOTHER vegetable burglary! Those thieves are unstoppable!"

"Don't worry, Dad," smiled Tom, hoping

that he wouldn't notice the runner bean hanging out of Mabel's mouth. "Now we have Mabel to protect your vegetables."

"But I haven't heard her bark once yet!" exclaimed Tom's dad. "I'm not sure she's going to be much of a guard dog after all."

Tom looked at Mabel. Now he came to think of it, he hadn't heard Mabel bark either – even when Mrs Peartree's cat had hissed at her.

Days went by, and Mabel still hadn't barked or done any tricks. Worse than that, she just kept growing and growing and growing!

One evening, Tom and his parents had just settled down to watch their favourite film when – "OOOOF!" squealed Tom's mum, as Mabel launched herself onto the sofa to join them.

"Get down, Mabel!" cried Tom's dad. "You're far too big to sit on our laps!"

"Mabel IS awfully big," said Tom's mum, sadly, as she tucked Tom into bed that night. "I'm not sure how much longer she'll be able to fit in the house! And she can't even bark, so it doesn't look like she'll be able to protect Dad's vegetables. Perhaps she's not quite the right dog for us. I've spoken to Dad and we think it's best if Mabel goes back to the rescue centre in the morning."

As Tom's mum turned the light out, Mabel gave Tom a very wet lick on his nose and curled up beside his bed. Tom sighed. Mabel might be ginormous and she might be a rubbish guard dog but she was his, and he couldn't possibly let her go back to the rescue centre!

Later that night, Tom woke to the sound of footsteps outside and a murmur of voices. He sat bolt upright in bed. Mabel was gone! Tom tiptoed to the kitchen. "Mabel?" he called.

Suddenly, there was a terrifying ROAR! Tom ran to the window to see . . .

. . . Mabel stomping and roaring! Trembling in front of her were two very scared-looking thieves, both clutching armfuls of his dad's vegetables!

"Yikes!" squealed one of the thieves, looking up at Mabel. "It's a monster!"

"That's not a monster!" shouted Tom from the window. "That's my . . ." He looked at Mabel again, and all of a sudden he understood. "That's my DINOSAUR!"

In a flash, two police officers appeared, just as Tom's mum and dad stumbled sleepily outside.

"Mum! Dad!" Tom cried as he raced outside to join them. "Mabel is a dinosaur, not a dog! She's a Stegosaurus! That's why she doesn't like steak and she can't bark!"

"Mabel's not just any old dinosaur," smiled one of the police officers, as they led the burglars away. "She's a top-notch GUARD-dinosaur! We've been trying to catch these vegetable thieves for months!"

Tom was allowed to keep Mabel after that, as everyone agreed that she really was an outstanding guard-dinosaur. Even though Mabel soon grew too big for Tom's house, she lived very happily in the garden. And after Tom's dad won first prize for his broccoli in the village vegetable competition, he gave Mabel her very own vegetable patch . . . and no vegetable thieves ever dared to come near the house again.

The Littlest Viking

Written by Lucy M. George

Illustrated by Erica Salcedo

The Littlest Viking

Troy whizzed around in the office chair next to his mum. "Are we going home soon?" he asked. "I'm hungry!"

"Nearly done," said Mum, looking up from her computer. "Why don't you go and see the dinosaur exhibition?"

"OK," said Troy, sliding off his chair and walking towards the door.

"I won't be long!" called his mum, typing furiously.

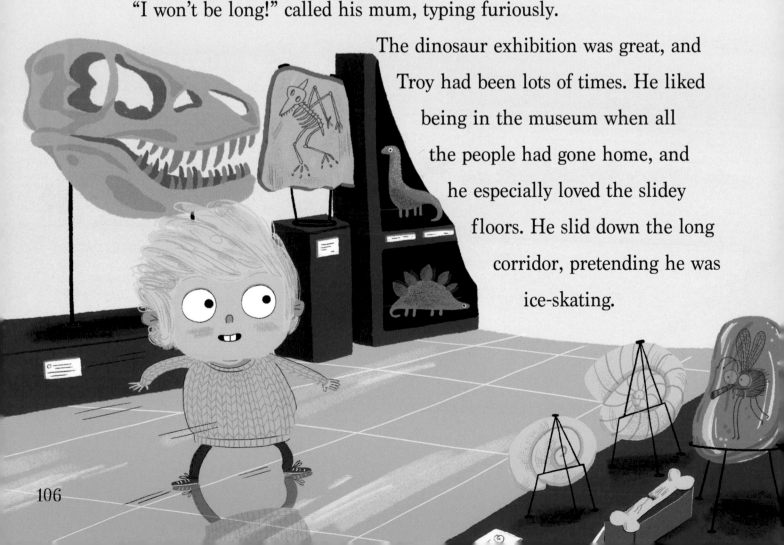

The dinosaur exhibition was great, and Troy had been lots of times. He liked being in the museum when all the people had gone home, and he especially loved the slidey floors. He slid down the long corridor, pretending he was ice-skating.

Halfway down the corridor, Troy noticed a huge wooden door standing wide open. He was sure it hadn't been there last week. He peeped inside and couldn't believe his eyes. The room was full of ancient costumes – gladiator armour, Egyptian masks and even pirate hats! But the thing that really caught Troy's eye was a shiny metal helmet with two horns. It looked like a Viking helmet! The sign read 'DO NOT TOUCH'.

"Wow," Troy whispered. He knew he shouldn't, but he really wanted to touch it. His mum had told him all about Vikings, and Troy had thought they sounded really cool! Perhaps he could just try it on quickly, and put it straight back.

Troy stood on his tiptoes and lifted the helmet, placing it on his head. All at once, darkness surrounded him and he felt himself falling through the air.

When he opened his eyes, the museum had gone and he was on a narrow cliff, looking across a green valley. "Where am I?" said Troy shakily. He looked down to find that his clothes had changed too. He looked just like a Viking! The helmet must be magic!

Troy looked around. He had to find his way back to the museum – his mum would be worried sick! A narrow path wound down the hillside, so Troy set off along it at a trot.

He walked and walked for what felt like hours. His legs were so tired. "What will Mum think when she realises I'm missing?" he thought, sadly, sitting down to rest. "I wonder if I'll ever get home again."

"What have we here?" said a voice from high above him. Troy looked up and saw a group of children a little older than him. They had helmets just like his, and they wore fur coats and leather belts. Vikings!

"Aren't you a bit young to be out here alone?" said one of the girls. "Where's your village?"

"I don't know," said Troy, his voice wobbling.

"Why don't you come along with us? We're going to be late for the boat race, but we can take you back after."

A boat race? That sounded fun. Troy raced toy boats across the duck pond in the park with his mum all the time, and he often won. He decided to tag along with the group.

"I'm Troy," he said, as they followed the path towards the sea. "What's your name?"

"Welcome to the team, Troy," replied the girl, smiling down at him. "I'm Erika."

As they walked round a bend they reached a bay filled with hundreds of huge longships, their sails billowing in the breeze. They hadn't meant toy boats at all – he was going to ride in a real Viking ship!

"Ready to row?" Erika shouted to the rest of the team.

"YEAH!" they cheered back.

Troy charged with them to their ship at the water's edge, and watched as they leapt in. "Come on, little Viking!" they cried, and many pairs of hands reached down to lift him onto the boat.

On board the Vikings quickly sat on wooden benches and took up their oars. Erika showed him to his place – next to her, at the very front!

"You can be our little mascot," said Erika. Troy grinned at her.

"You'll bring us luck!" said the blonde boy beside him, slapping him on the shoulder. Just then a deafening noise filled the bay as someone blew a horn. The race had begun!

The Vikings began to move their oars through the water, pulling and pushing in rhythm. Huge waves crashed around them as the Vikings sang a loud song.

"We're over halfway!" shouted Erika. "But we're not in the lead yet!" The Vikings put on a burst of speed, and Troy watched in awe as the sails belonging to the other boats began to drop behind. He could see the finish line – but in their path lay a huge rock, and the Vikings didn't seem to have seen it!

"Steer left!" shouted Troy. "We're going to crash!" The crew reacted at once, rowing with all their might. The boat turned, *just* missing the rock!

"We've won!" cried Erika, as they sped past the finish flag. The friends erupted in cheers.

Troy beamed as everyone slapped him on the back. "It was all thanks to our mini Viking!" they cried.

Back on dry land, they shared a great feast. There was warm bread, hot soup in wooden bowls, and barbequed meats and fish. "I love being a Viking!" said Troy, as they tucked into the delicious food.

"You're funny!" laughed Erika. "Our funny, lucky, little Viking." She raised her cup. "To Troy!"

"TROY!" everyone shouted, knocking their wooden cups.

It had been a truly amazing day. Troy smiled sleepily at his new friends. The sea air and the food had tired him out. He decided to rest his head on the table just for a moment . . .

But as he did so, he felt the helmet slowly slide from his head. It clattered to the floor, and Troy felt cold air rush around him.

He was back in the museum! The Viking helmet was back on its stand in front of him. Troy stared at the 'DO NOT TOUCH' sign. Just then he heard footsteps behind him.

"There you are, Troy, I was worried!" said his mum. "I've been looking for you everywhere!"

"Sorry, Mum," said Troy, hugging her. "It's good to see you!"

Mum hugged him back, surprised.

"I've had an amazing time!" he said.

"Well, great!" said Mum. "Now let's go home. I hope you don't mind coming in with me again tomorrow?"

"No," said Troy, beaming, "I'd love to!"

Sophie At Sea

Written by Becky Davies

Illustrated by Sue Eastland

Sophie At Sea

"Wow!" said Sophie. "Look, Aunt Jane. Dolphins!" She leaned over the railing of the *Victoria*, giggling as the wind whipped sea spray over her head.

"I'm glad you like sailing, Sophie," laughed Aunt Jane. "It's still a long way to Brazil!"

"Will Mum and Dad meet us straight away?" Sophie asked eagerly. Her parents were animal researchers, and often worked in faraway places.

"Yes, they can't wait to see you!" said Aunt Jane. "Now let's go inside, this sea air is chilly!"

"Can I explore the ship?" Sophie asked. There were no other children on the *Victoria*, so Sophie had become used to playing on her own.

"Of course dear, just don't go on deck without me."

Sophie hadn't gone far when she came across a trap door set into the floor. "What's in here?" she wondered, lifting it to reveal a wooden ladder. She climbed down carefully, and found herself in a warm room that smelt of hay. "Horses!" she exclaimed. "How wonderful!"

Sophie walked down the row of stables, looking eagerly at the horses and stroking their velvety noses. Just then, a small dog burst from the last stable and leapt at her, wagging his tail. "Hello!" said Sophie. "Aunt Jane would love you! Now you wait here, I'll go get her."

"Wait!" someone hissed.

"Who was that?" asked Sophie, looking around in surprise.

"Me!" said the voice.

It was a small boy, who Sophie now saw had been curled up in the hay.

"Hello, I'm Sophie. Who are you?" she said.

The boy stood, scooping the dog into his arms.

"I'm Robert," he said. "And this is Alfie."

Sophie thought he looked rather dirty, and quite young to be by himself on the ship.

"What are you doing down here?" she asked.

"I snuck on board. I've been hiding."

Sophie gasped. "Where are your parents?"

"Haven't got any," Robert shrugged.

"Nowhere to live either. Please don't tell anyone I'm here, I'll get into trouble!"

"No parents? How awful," said Sophie.

"I won't tell, Robert. Do you want some chocolate?"

Sophie began visiting Robert and Alfie every day. He and the small dog were inseparable, and Robert seemed to understand everything that Alfie did! He loved animals even more than she did, and when Sophie took him the special books her parents had sent, he looked eagerly at the pictures of tropical birds and creatures.

They were so absorbed in these books one day that they didn't hear the trap door being lifted. "There you are, Sophie!" said a voice. It was Aunt Jane. "And who is this?"

Aunt Jane was kind to Robert, but insisted that they all go and speak to the Captain at once. "You should have told me straight away, dear," she said, knocking on the Captain's cabin door. "The Captain won't be pleased."

The Captain *wasn't* pleased. "This ship is no place for a little boy," he said, sternly. "Who will look after him?"

"Please let him stay!" said Sophie. "Aunt Jane will look after him, won't you?" she looked at her aunt pleadingly.

Aunt Jane looked from Sophie to Robert.

"Alright then, Robert. You can stay with us until we get to Brazil. You and Alfie may share our cabin."

"Just make sure he stays out of trouble," grumbled the Captain.

Robert was overjoyed, and skipped the whole way to the stables to fetch Alfie. But as they got closer to Brazil, Robert's happiness began to fade and Sophie was worried. What would happen when they got there? He'd be on his own again. How terrible!

Then one day there came a shout from one of the crew. He had spotted a desert island with a huge mountain at its centre.

The Captain agreed that everyone could do with a rest, so they were all allowed to go ashore!

Sophie and Robert raced on to the white sand, Alfie at their heels. "Wow!" Sophie cried. The island was the most beautiful thing either of them had ever seen. They had a wonderful day spotting multi-coloured birds, playing with the soft sand and splashing in the shallows with Aunt Jane. As the sun set the three of them sat together, drinking from delicious coconuts.

Just then, Alfie let out a whimper. "What is it, boy?" said Robert, listening intently. The birds had fallen silent and even the insects had stopped chirping! Robert held his breath and waited, but the silence went on. Alfie whined again and pawed at his arm. "Aunt Jane . . ." said Robert. "Something's wrong."

"What do you mean?" said Aunt Jane, looking up.

"Listen. I think the animals are trying to warn us!"

Aunt Jane and Sophie listened, their eyes widening when they noticed the silence. "You're right!" cried Sophie.

Aunt Jane's eyes settled on the mountain. "We need to get back to the ship. That's no mountain – it's a volcano, and I think it's going to erupt!"

They raced back to the ship, shouting and waving their arms. "Captain!" cried Robert. "We have to go right NOW! There's a volcano on this island!"

"It's true," panted Aunt Jane. "It's going to erupt! Robert spotted the warning signs!"

The Captain looked at Robert, then looked at the volcano. Smoke was rising high into the air. "Clever boy!" he murmured in surprise. Then he bellowed, "All hands on deck!" and the crew came running.

As the anchor was lifted there was a mighty rumble from the volcano. The crew and passengers gasped. "Robert is a hero!" someone cried, and everyone cheered.

"You saved us all," said the Captain, patting Robert on the back. Robert beamed with happiness, and Sophie squeezed his hand.

When at last the ship reached Brazil, Sophie ran straight into the arms of her waiting parents.

"Oh darling, it's so good to see you! We've missed you!" cried her mum.

"You too!" beamed Sophie, as she and Aunt Jane hugged her parents.

"Mum, Dad, there's someone you need to meet." She beckoned to Robert, who had been waiting shyly a few paces behind with Alfie. Sophie told her parents all about him and what had happened with the volcano.

"He saved us!" said Sophie "Please don't let him go back to England on his own."

"He's a very intelligent boy," smiled Aunt Jane.

"Well, Robert," said Sophie's dad, shaking Robert's hand. "It sounds like we have a lot to thank you and Alfie for. With your skills, we'd be silly not to keep you around. How does a job as official family protector sound?"

Robert grinned. He'd have to check with Alfie, but he thought that would be just grand.

Bethany Bear's Big Mystery

Written by Amelia Hepworth

Illustrated by Chris Jevons

Bethany Bear's Big Mystery

It was Bethany Bear's birthday and she was having a picnic with her friends. There were brightly coloured balloons, jam sponge and piles of presents. The very last present was from Bethany's mum and dad.

"I wonder what it is?" whispered Sammy Squirrel as Bethany pulled off the wrapping paper. Inside was a small red case and written on the front were the words . . .

DETECTIVE KIT: ALL YOU NEED TO BE A SUPER SLEUTH

It contained super spyglasses and a magnifying glass that made everything bigger. There was even a special kit for taking fingerprints!

"Wow!" said Bethany's friend, Molly Mouse. "You're so lucky – that's the best present EVER!"

Bethany grinned and hugged her parents. "Thanks Mum, thanks Dad! I can't wait to be a detective."

Later, in Bethany's bedroom, the three friends took turns using the magnifying glass and trying on the glasses.

"Now we just need something to detect!" said Sammy excitedly.

"Don't worry, there's bound to be mysteries everywhere," said Bethany. "Let's meet back here tomorrow morning and see what we've found."

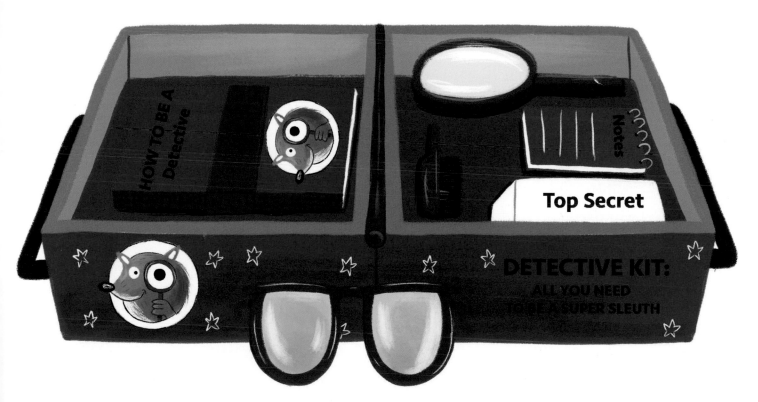

The next day when Sammy arrived he was clutching a bag of cookies. "I found Mrs Crabapple's cat," he explained. "She was stuck up a tree. I was looking for clues in the garden when I heard her miaowing. Mrs Crabapple says I'm an excellent detective. She gave me these cookies to say thank you. Would you like one?"

"That's great!" mumbled Bethany through a mouthful of crumbs. "What about you, Molly?"

"I found my dad's glasses for him," replied Molly. "They had fallen down the back of the sofa and he couldn't see a thing! He was very happy that I discovered them with my detecting."

Bethany crunched thoughtfully on the last bit of her cookie. It was very unfair that nothing had happened at her house. It was *her* detective set after all!

Later that day, after Bethany had spent the whole morning looking for clues, she finally gave up and sat down to do some drawing at the kitchen table. She was just gazing out of the window trying to think what to draw, when suddenly she noticed something. The old, broken swing that usually hung from the apple tree had disappeared!

A real mystery at last! Bethany raced to her bedroom and grabbed her detective kit. Then she hurried out to search for clues.

Bethany looked and looked but she couldn't find anything. The swing was just *gone*. Then, just as she was about to give up, she spotted something glinting in the sunlight. "A marble!" whispered Bethany, examining it with her magnifying glass. "It must belong to whoever took the swing."

When Bethany told her friends about the mystery of the missing swing they were very excited. "Let's look for more clues!" squeaked Molly. So while Bethany dusted the marble for fingerprints, the others set to work combing the area.

Before long, Molly found a footprint in the flowerbed nearest the swing. They took turns looking at it through the spyglasses and sketched it in Bethany's notebook.

The friends carried on detecting all afternoon until they were tired out. After supper Bethany went straight up to her bed, yawning sleepily. "Maybe I'll find some more clues tomorrow," she thought to herself before falling fast asleep.

But when Bethany wandered down to breakfast the next morning, the swing was back! And it was shiny and mended – with bright red paint and sturdy new ropes. The thief hadn't stolen it at all – they'd fixed it!

Molly and Sammy couldn't believe it when they heard the news. "Yippee!" cried Sammy, jumping on and swinging as high as he could go. "Whoever did this must be very clever."

"Yes," agreed Bethany. "But I still wish we knew who it was so we could thank them."

Over the next few days the friends were on the lookout for more clues. And each morning they found more and more footprints. "Whoever fixed the swing must be visiting at night," concluded Bethany.

"We could have a sleepover," suggested Molly, "and keep watch!"

"Yes!" agreed Sammy. "But what if we fall asleep and miss them?"

"I know," replied Bethany. "We'll tie something noisy to the ropes. That way we'll definitely wake up. That's what a proper detective would do."

So the three friends tied Bethany's mum's windchimes tightly onto the swing, and snuggled up in Bethany's bed to wait.

"I hope we find the mystery visitor!" said Molly who was trying hard to stay awake. But the bed was so cosy and before long the three friends started drifting off to sleep.

Then all of a sudden, Bethany woke with a jump. There was a tinkling noise coming from the garden. The windchimes! She raced to the window, calling to the others to wake them up.

Bethany peered out of the window and saw . . . a family of badgers! The littlest badger was laughing and swinging back and forth, kicking his feet. The friends rushed out to say hello.

"We're your new neighbours," said Mrs Badger, "and this is Billy. I hope you don't mind him using your swing?"

"Of course not!" said Bethany. Just then she noticed some red paint on Billy's scarf. It perfectly matched the shiny swing.

"Aha!" she cried, delighted to have solved the mystery at last. "It was *you* who fixed the swing, wasn't it?"

Billy nodded, blushing shyly. "I like fixing things. And I thought you could use the swing in the day time and I could use it at night."

Bethany grinned. She thought this sounded very clever indeed. "I think I have something of yours," she said. And she handed Billy the shiny marble.

"My marble!" exclaimed Billy. "Thank you! I thought I had lost that."

They took turns playing on the swing until, yawning, the three friends waved goodbye to Billy and returned to bed. "Being a detective is brilliant," mumbled Bethany before she fell fast asleep. "And I'm going to solve an even bigger mystery tomorrow."

Favourite Adventure Stories
An Illustrated Treasury

LITTLE TIGER PRESS LTD
an imprint of the Little Tiger Group
1 Coda Studios, 189 Munster Road,
London SW6 6AW
www.littletiger.co.uk

Published in Great Britain 2017
This volume copyright © Little Tiger Press 2016
Cover illustration by Tim Budgen
Text and illustrations copyright © Little Tiger Press 2016

Printed in China
ISBN 978-1-84869-417-0
LTP/2700/1964/0917
2 4 6 8 10 9 7 5 3